OZZY the Ostrich

JOSÉ CARLOS ANDRÉS

BEA ENRÍQUEZ

nubeOCHO

Trotting across the plain,
Ozzy the ostrich found **a flower.**

She looked at it,
sniffed it,
and ate it all up.

YUM!

Trotting across the plain,
two ostriches found **two flowers.**

They looked at them,
sniffed them,
and ate them all up.

YUM!

YUM!

Trotting across the plain,
three ostriches found **three** flowers.

They looked at them,
sniffed them,
and ate them all up.

YUM! YUM! YUM!

Trotting across the plain,
a lion saw **an ostrich**,
licked his lips,
and thought: *YUM!*

YUM!

Trotting across the plain,
two lions saw **two ostriches**,
licked their lips and their noses and
teeth, and thought: *YUM! YUM!*

Trotting across the plain,
three lions saw **three** ostriches,
licked their lips and their whiskers and
claws, and thought: *YUM! YUM! YUM!*

YUM!

All of a sudden, **Ozzy** ran off
and hid behind some bushes.

Ozzy came back with **an egg** and said:
"Look! I'm going to be a mother!"

The three ostriches sang and danced with joy.

All of a sudden the birds spied the lions and yelled with fear:

"They're going to eat us!"

The lions roared:

"We're going to eat you!"

Ozzy, protecting the egg under her wing, said:

"Nah-nana-naa-nah...
Not you, nor you, nor
you can get this egg!

Just then, the **king** of the pride gave **a grunt** and the lions charged after their prey.

Ozzy whistled and the big birds buried their heads in the sand.

The **three lions** surrounded the **three ostriches** (and the egg)
They looked at them, licked their lips and their manes and
tails, and thought: *YUM!*

Ozzy, with her head in the sand, thought:
Nah-nana-naa-nah... Not you, nor you, nor you
can get this egg!

She whistled again and the birds,
pulling their heads out of the sand, **yelled:**

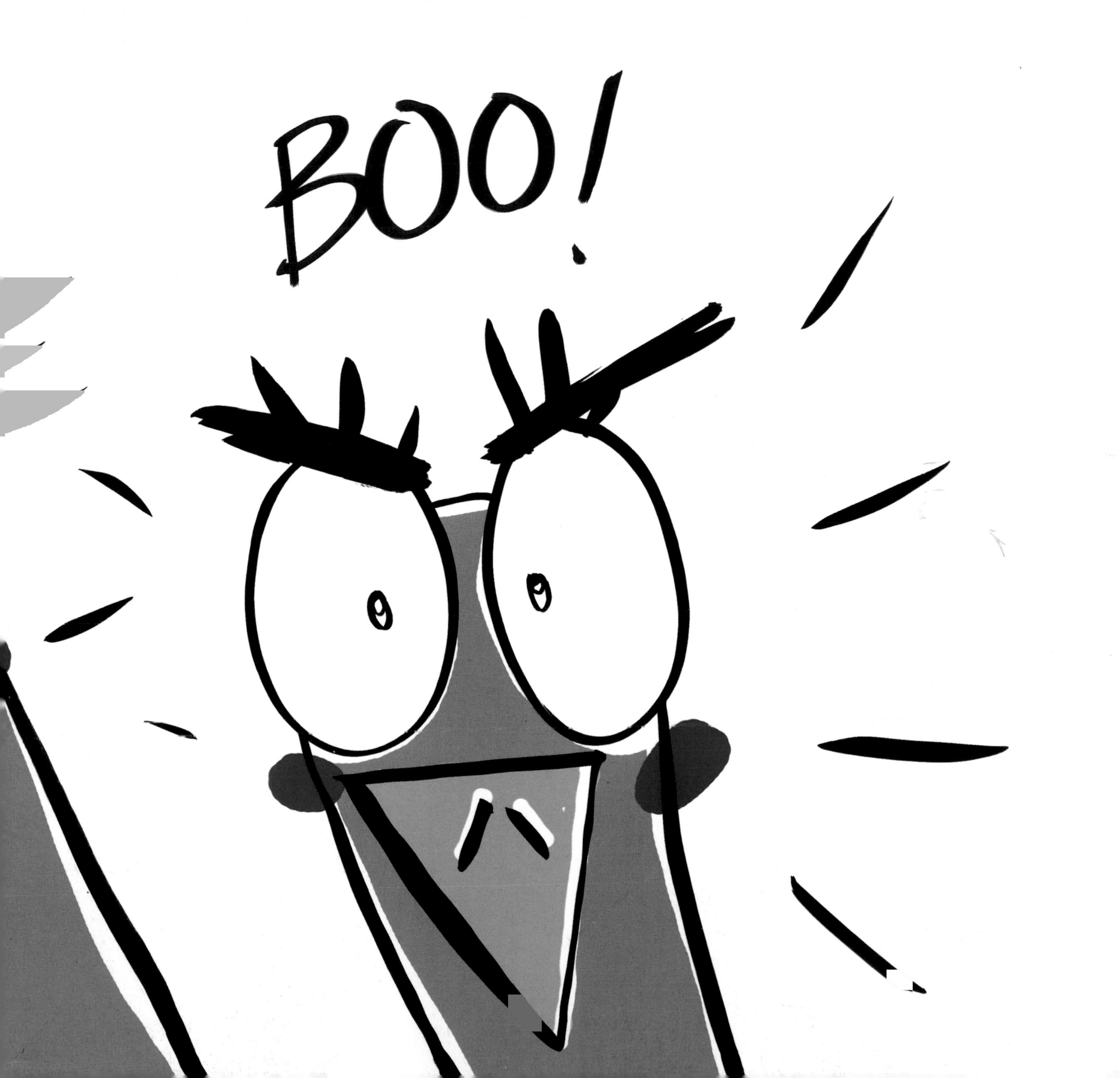
BOO!

One lion got so scared that he turned **white.**
Another lost all of his **fur.**
And the third one's **teeth** fell out.

The ostriches sang:
"Nah-nana-naa-nah... Not you, nor you,
nor you can get this egg!"
And the lions ran away as fast as they could.

The three lions were trotting across the plain, when the **toothless one** found **a flower,** sniffed it and because he could eat nothing else, ate it all up.

The one who had lost all of his **fur** found some **feathers** and made a rather fetching wig with them.

And the white one, **whiter** than an **ostrich egg,**
found a **rainbow** and (because he had no color),
he put it on as a **coat.**

The **three ostriches** (and the **egg**) met the **three lions** who looked stranger than a pink elephant. They looked at each other, **sniffed** each other, and became **friends.**

Another pride of lions saw the **three ostriches** (and the **egg**) with the **three lions** who looked stranger than a purple unicorn. They looked at them, sniffed them, and licked their lips.

CRACK!!!

Just then the egg **cracked** open.